Tere Bina Tanha Yahan

Flairs and Glairs
Publication House

"Tere Bina Tanha Yahan"

ISBN No: " 978-93-90416-85-1"

1st Edition

Language – English and Hindi

Flairs and Glairs

Publication House

Regd. Under MSME Act.

Disclaimer

This is a work of fiction and solely represent the thoughts of the corresponding authors of the articles. Our editors have tried their best to edit the content of all the authors and check the plagiarism.
All the write-ups in this book are unique and are only published in this book.
In case any plagiarism or error is found, only the author is responsible alone, and not the publisher or the Compilers.

Cover Designing and Book Formatting
Shubham Shah

Acknowledgement

Dear Almighty, thank you for blessing me with the power and zeal to be able to complete this Anthology. Also, Thank You dear parents, for trusting in me, and letting me work whenever I wanted. My family is the one who supported me for what I am today.
When it comes to this Anthology, I would like to start with Thanking the Co-authors, without your help and support, I would have never been able to complete it.

Thank You all of you, for being there. Much Love to all of You. I am glad to see you all standing by me.

Co Authors

Shubham Shah (Founder Flairs and Glairs)
Ishani Agarwal (Founder Flairs and Glairs)
Shivangi Jaiswal (Compiler)

1. Jyoti Singh Rajput
2. Nishiket R Surwade
3. Heena Shaikh Mulla
4. Shivansh Sharma
5. Deepjyoti Chowdhury
6. Ayesha Rajpal
7. Shaily Tyagi
8. Bickey Mandal
9. Sourav Bhatia
10. Mausam Agrawal
11. Alina Tamkanat
12. Arijit Mondal
13. Suhita S
14. Saloni Lal Srivastava
15. Pragya Verma
16. Akanksha Sinha
17. अनिल विश्वकर्मा
18. Mohua Chakraborty
19. Sachin Banoudhiya
20. Shresth Bhargava
21. Meenakshi Sharma
22. Mansi Kanungo
23. Parwana Bibi
24. Muskan Gupta

25.Hynul Jaseena
26.पुलिन भारती
27.Puja kundu
28.Shobha Rajpal
29.Priyanshi Kamboj
30.Anisha Panda
31.Smriti Kumari
32.Dwiza
33.Shweta Rajput
34.Avi Srivastava
35.Hida Naz
36.Komal Surwade
37.Lokesh Upadhyay.
38.Raghav laximan Gawde
39.Aditya Srivastava
40.Maitreyee
41.Adarsh Kumar Priyadarshi
42.Sanjida Khan
43.Vanshika Gupta
44.Nelofer Talukdar
45.Saloni Santosh Gawas
46.Reshmi Vernekar
47.Vaishnavi Naik
48.Payal Singhal
49.Saheb Ghosh
50.Bushra Shaikh

Shubham Shah

(Founder- Flairs and Glairs)

Shubham Shah, entrepreneur at "Flairs & Glairs" a brand with dynamics in events organizing and cultural educational pan INDIA, He is a 26yr. old guy who recently has entered, the digital platform of imprinting emotions. He has initiated with his own open mic platform to help budding poets and aspiring writers under his brand named as "Teekhe Zasbaaat"
He is a commerce graduate from Bhagalpur City of Bihar.
He says Writing has impersonated him since childhood and he has now been writing for over a decade!
Cooking, on the other hand, is his passion! He also mentions, trying out new things just tickles him!

When asked sir, Why SPICY EMOTIONS?
He smiled and added, "agar jasbaat teekhe na ho toh wo jasbaat kaha" Spices are all that blends! So do his words!
As a chef, he presents to you his dish! Hot and freshly served! Taste it! Feel it! Enjoy it! You can also find his writing in the Solo book "Teekhe Zasbaaat" and 70+ anthologies. With his passion to explore opportunities across Platforms he is working with keen devotion and We wish him all the very best for his future ventures
Share your reviews on his

INSTAGRAM

@spicy_emotions
@shubham4shah

Or via email on

shubham2shah@gmail.com

To stay tuned to his work and opportunities follow his business Handles

INSTAGRAM FACEBOOK YOUTUBE

@flairsandglairs
@teekhezasbaaat

WEBSITE:

https://flairsandglairs.in/
https://flairsandglairs.com/

Ishani Agarwal

(Co Founder- Flairs and Glairs)

Ishani Agarwal
Born and brought up in Kolkata, she has done her schooling and college from here itself. She is doing her post-graduation at the moment. Ishani loves talking to people around, and is excited for this new beginning of hers! Been a Compiler for 35+ Anthologies, and in the process for more, also, co-authored in 100+ Anthologies, Ishani is very Happy with how her life is turning out now!
Insta handle: Ishani_agarwal_quotes

Shivangi Jaiswal

(Compiler)

Shivangi Jaiswal is a Content Writer from Kolkata. Project Head & Coordinator at "Flairs & Glairs" brand with dynamics in events organizing and cultural educational pan INDIA. Organiser at "The Glittering Fables" Writing Community. She is a B.Com Honours graduate. Certified in

Stocks & Short Selling as well as Certified in Digital Marketing Been a keen student, she has recently been Certified for learning Spanish Language..She loves to bring smiles and happiness to many faces, so she is into social service. Shivangi has also done her Diploma in painting, drawing and all kinds of clay making, craft works. Traveler, Teacher, Meditator, Dancer, Singer, Instrument Player. She loves to play guitar and harmonium. Been a public speaker she has taken part in many events and nailed it. Also been a great Advisor to many. Sports freak of Swimming and Badminton with a passion so strong. Since, past one year she has started her writing journey. She writes so that many people can connect with their stories and get positive hopes. She thinks " Every story is unique so embrace yourself to the best".She is a writer by day and a reader by night. Been a Complier of 20+ Anthologies, and in process for more, also Co- authored 70+ anthologies. Shivangi is an old soul with young eyes, a vintage heart, and a beautiful mind."

You can follow her work:

Instagram

@the_knockingvibe

@house_of_compilations

A Soldier Love

Goodbye, I'll be back soon.
He says while he was leaving.
Kissing her forehead saying "Take care",
He heading towards the car.
Not knowing when he would be back.

Fighting for the nation
Facing all the dangers,
Hit hard he knew he was not well
Still he kept his spirits high.
To win and survive for her motherland.

A strong woman was praying
for his love's life.
Waiting for his love to come home.
Every day she stands near the door.

Months, Years Passed
She kept faith for her love to return
As she was a brave woman of a strong man.
He is there, she is here.
A thousand miles apart.
They made a long-distance love.

Love is not always meant to be live together.
Some love stories are way beyond love
Because Faith and Trust is a root of a love tree.

Waiting.

All alone lying under the sky
Waiting to see you soon

Counting each and every minute
to pass soon.

Sadness all i feel missing you a lot
Wishing you were beside me..

Really wanted to see you
But don't know what to do?

May be someday I'll definitely meet you
And that day I can't wait to come..

The connection between us is so pure,
I feel it always.

No matter how far we are
The spark of our love will always
stay strong..

Because I know One day
this distance will disappear
And we will be back with
Our Love & Light Spark.

Separate Ways.

Sometimes we never realise the value
of love until distance is created...
Until the final goodbye.
I didn't know my heart would feel the pain
Without you that day.

The day you left,
This distance gave me a heavy pain
As my heart cried till the dawn
Remembering the last smile, you gave away.

I believe that love grows in Distance,
But with time it makes us go in our
two separate ways.
Truly and madly in Love
Pain and Heart breaks is all meant in Distance.

Jyoti Singh Rajput

Jyoti Singh Rajput is a banker by profession and marks the ink, as her passion. She believes, the pen holded with passion, has power to bring change and it even emote the emotions, that can't be verbally exchanged and are left unsaid. She is also a lyricist, a nature lover, an enthusiast contributing to welfare works and urges all to help those who needs, as she says, we are human for good deeds. A multilingual and a promising poet, Jyoti Singh Rajput has worked in many books of different genres. She is a basket of masterpieces and her poetry sheds stories, some of love and the memories, some of those tinch and the waving worries, some of life and it's theories. You can follow her on
instagram @ the_frozen_flame_2801,
and on yourquote @ Jyoti - the frozen flame for her more write ups.

तेरी यादों से नाता कुछ ऐसा गेहरा है

तेरी यादों से नाता कुछ ऐसा गेहरा है
कि मेरी हर धड़कन पर आज भी सिर्फ तेरा पेहरा है
मेरी ज़िन्दगी की कहानी में आए कई किरदार मगर
जेहन में आज भी सिर्फ तेरा चेहरा है
तेरी यादों से ही होता रौशन मेरा हर सवेरा है
मेरी रूह में आज भी सिर्फ तेरा ही बसेरा है
वो चांदनी रात आज भी ख्वाबों सा सुनेहरा है
तेरे इश्क का इत्र आज भी मेरी सांसों में बेह रहा है
वक़्त आज भी उस लम्हें में ठेहरा है
तेरी यादों से नाता कुछ ऐसा गेहरा है...

Nishiket R Surwade

Mr.Nishiket R Surwade,born on 24th july 1999 .
He is a student pursuing his engineering in electronics and telecommunication field ,Nashik, Maharashtra.
He is very shy and simple, easily make friends.
He is a blogger and future E&TC engineer.
He aspires to become IAS Officer.
He started writing as a career since he was in 12th std.
He loves to write quote and shayri in Hindi as well as in english language.
He loves to write about 'True love'
He worked as co-author in some anthologies like 'The Broken Bond',
'For the name of love' and in more than 25 Anthologies. and also Being a compiler of the book College Romance ,Life Sahi Hai and many are in process

Duriyan

Lambi hai duri
279 km
Lag jayege 60 ghante
Lekin kise padi hai..

Jiss tarah mujhe mohabbat hai,
Ussi tarah tumhe bhi mujhse hai,
Toh kai hum alag nahi hai ,
Itne milon ke bawjood..

Tum aur main dur hoke hai,
Lekin dil se pass hai,
Mann ko duriya mayne nahi rakhti,
Aur dil ko duri ki parwah nahin.

Hum mohabbat main hai,
Duriyon main,
Hum hamesha mohabbat krenge,
Duriyon main bhi.

Bhale hi hum dur hai,
Par hamara dil to sath hai,
Haan mohabbat hai ,
Duriyon main bhi...

Mulakat

Socha nahi tha kabhi iss zindgi main aisa bhi ek pal aayga jo humse dur ho kar dil ke sabse karib hoga ....

Shivansh Sharma

He is shivansh sharma . Basically from indore but persuing MBA(Marketing &Hr) in mysore karnataka . He always have passion towards writng the thoughts which comes in to his mind . A hardcore fodiee as he belongs to indore . He is the one who is always ready to help to his near ones .His life revolves around his family and friends. He is always self motivated , enthusiastic and person with positive vibes .He is co-author of 10+ books and compiler of 1 book . His only belief is just live happily and enjoy every moment of life .

You can contact him on ig@shivanshrockzzzzz

प्यार और दूरियां

दूर रहकर भी तुमसे मोहब्बत करना
यह मोहब्बत कहीं आधी तो नहीं है ,
हमारे प्यार के अफसाने के लिए
तुम पास रहो मेरे यह ज़रूरी नहीं है,
तुम्हे भले बहुत समय से देखा नहीं है
तुम्हे महसूस हर समय किया है ,
तुम्हे काफी समय से
अपनी बाहों में भरा नहीं है ,
तुम्हारी गोद में सिर रखकर
सोया नहीं हूं ,
लोग सवाल उठाते है ,
मेरी दीवानगी पर ,
की तेरे पास नहीं है ,
फिर भी इतना प्यार करता क्यूं है ,
बात तो यह सही है ,
मेरी हर तम्माना पूरी नहीं हुई है ,
प्यार करने के लिए हर वक़्त
साथ रहो मेरे यह भी ज़रूरी नहीं है ,

माना हर बात तुम्हे बता नहीं पाता ,
पास बैठकर अपने दिल की
धड़कन सुना नहीं पता ,
अब तो यह दूरियां सताने लगी है मुझे ,
पर भी मेरे प्यार में कोई कमी नहीं है,
बहुत समय से कोई दिन ,
तेरे साथ बिताया नहीं है ,
पर इन दूरियों में भी हमारी
नजदीकियां कम नहीं हुई है ,
इतना भी गम नहीं है ,
तेरे दूर होने का ,
तुझे में आंख बंद करके महसूस
करता हूं हर वक़्त मेरे पास ,
दूर हो जाऊं में तुझसे ,
इन फासलों में इतना दम नहीं है ,
एक दिन हम होंगे एक साथ ,
याद करेंगे यह दूरी वाला प्यार
साथ बैठकर , मेरे कंधे पे सिर रखकर
तुम बैठोगी और में तेरी जुल्फों
की छांव में गुम हो सा हो जाऊंगा ,
तुमसे प्यार करने के लिए पास रहो मेरे

यह हर वक़्त ज़रूरी नहीं है ।।।

Heena Shaikh Mulla

Heena Shaikh Mulla is from Pune,currently residing in Karnataka.
She's from an ICSE background,graduated from Pune University(MSC Computer Science). She's the author of 'Technical Desserts' and also holds a Vajra record for the same.

Besides being a college topper,She likes drawing henna,teaching and fantasizes about Polar Bears.

She's a charming personality who expresses her thoughts in the form of Poetry and Shayri and currently she's compiling books as well.

Muskurate Aansu

Zindagi me kuch pal bade aanokhe hote hai,
Koi hasate hai, toh koi rulate hai.

Par aise bhi kuch lamhe hote hai,
Jo laabo par muskaan aur aankho me aansu chod jate hai.

Phir chahe beti ki bidaai ho,
Ya bete ki videsh wali naukri.

Dil me khushi ki lehar k saath saath,
Bichadne ka gam bhi de jate hai.

Ye muskurate aansu,
Kamiyabi k saath saath, gehare ghaav bhi de jate hai..

Deepjyoti Chowdhury

Deepjyoti Chowdhury embraces reading and writing as her escape from the real world as well as a window to it. She is a strong believer of Christ and Karma. Written in 100+ anthologies, she is the author of Heartfelt musings and The staircase to freedom. Her main aim is to heal people and make them smile through her art of writing. You can follow her on Instagram at dj_writes_to_heal .

Distance

Since forever heard about long distance love story,
Never imagined it will create such a blissful memory.

I remember in the school corridor when our eyes met,
You walked away not noticing with an upright head.

I knew you were my studious and reserved senior,
As your beautiful eyes looked quite familiar.

While scrolling facebook when I saw you were my suggested friend,
Immediately without a thought a request to you was sent.

You took exactly five days to think and respond,
Within weeks of chatting, to each other we were fond.

Exact six months later you proposed me,
My heart was full of joy and was beating heavily.

From then till now five years have passed,
Every hurdle and storm together we have surpassed.

From a lover to fiance happily you promoted,
Our true love by our parents was supported.

Happily inking this as our wedding would soon take place,
Distance doesn't matter, if true love we truthfully embrace.

Ayesha Rajpal

Ayesha Rajpal is writer by passion. She is into nobel profession of teaching and runs an academy in Delhi. She is fun lovung and easy going person and has been co author for few books . She is into writing poems . Even she loves calligraphy and Mandala art too.

Heart Grows Fonder

Distance never matters
What matters to me is you
You live near to me or far
But I will find you always near to my heart
My eyes keep searching for you
My heart just wants to be with you
The only place I feel safe
Is just with you
Distance never matters
What matters to me is you

Shaily Tyagi

She is Shaily Tyagi, a born writer.
She is always ready to face challenges and gives her best in every field.
She is a compiler, loves to compile different feelings of different hearts.
Here she is with her beautiful poem, hope all will love to read.

तेरे बिन

क्या कहूं किसी से क्यों परेशान हूं मैं,
देखकर रंग इस बदलती दुनिया का हैरान हूं मैं।
किसको समझे अपना,
कौन है पराया,
अब नहीं है किसी पर भी यकीन,
झूठा लगता है मुझे अपना ही साया,
ना जाने क्यों फिर ,
किसी पर यकीन करने को दिल करता है,
देख लोगों की झूठी हंसी,
नकली चेहरे, ना जाने क्यों यह दिल डरता है,
क्या कहूं किसी से क्यों परेशान हूं मैं,
देखकर रंग बदलती दुनिया का हैरान हूं मैं।
पग-पग पर यहां लोग झूठे और मक्कार हैं,
जो दिखते हैं सीधे-साधे ,
असल में वही बड़े फनकार है,
हर लेते हैं खुद अपने ही अपनों को,
ना जाने निभा रहे कौन सा किरदार है।
क्या कहूं किसी से क्यों परेशान हूं मैं,
देखकर रंग बदलती दुनिया का हैरान हूं मैं।

Bickey Mandal

He is Bickey Mandal from Jharkhand. Now he is in the last semester of his graduation from B.B.M.K.U Dhanbad with English Honours. With his poetries he trying to connect himself with others. He is passionate about his works because he love what he do. He have a stedy source of motivations that drives him to do his best. He wants to became a writer from last 5 year so, he collect his Thoughts, Poetry and Lyrics from then to make a good book in his both books he presenting many beautiful shayari, Love quotes , Motivational quotes & sad stories. You can contact him through instagram at @bickey_ki_ankahi_baatein

E-mail- bickeymandal91@gmail.com

हमसफ़र का आस

हम सफर में रहे
हमसफ़र ना मिला
हम उसकी राह पे खड़ा
उसकी आस में रहे
ये उसे खबर ना मिला

तेरे लौट आने का खुशी
और दूर जाने का गम
तेरे संग जितना जियु
लगे मुझे उतना ही कम
करो एक वादा ऐसा
ना भूलने वाला जैसा

जिंदगी अब हर
मोड़ पर रुलाती है
बस तेरी और तेरी
याद दिलाती है

Sourav Bhatia

I am a song writer,composer and singer & shayar also

एक महोबत ऐसी भी

माना कि हम दूर हैं,माना कि हम मजबूर हैं पर इन दूरियों ने हमें और करीब लाया है

तो ही हमें ये महोबत मंजूर है।

वो इन्सान ही क्या जिसे प्यार ही ना हो,वो इन्सान ही क्या जिसे इकरार ना हो, और क्या मजा उस महोबत में जहां बेसब्री से मिलने का इंतजार ही ना हो

दूर रहकर दिल बस उसी के ख्यालों में खोया रहता है, क्या कर रही होगी, कैसे रहती होगी, क्या मुझे याद करती होगी, बस ये ही सब उट - पटांग कहता रहता है

ऐसे बन्धन में अंदर से बस एक ही आवाज आ रही होती है और ज्यादा फर्क नहीं होता ऐसी महोतब में ,बस उसकी बहां और मेरी यहां जान जा रही होती है।

(2)

सो सवाल उठ खड़े होते हैं जब वो एक दिन भी बात ना करे तो पर असल में देखा जाए तो ये ही सच्चा प्यार है और ऐसी महोबत करने वालों के लिए वो ही उसकी जिंदगी और वो ही याद होता है।

जितनी दूरी हो उतना प्यार बढ़ता है और जितनी दूरी हो उतना इंतजार बढ़ता है।

और एक अलग सी मुस्कान होती है दोनों के चेहरे पर जब बारी मिलने की आती है जैसे एक फूल के खिलने की आती है।

ऐसे एहसास जैसा एहसास कोई और हो नहीं सकता और अगर नहीं होता मेरा महबूब मुझसे इतना दूर तो शायद कभी इतना प्यार ही नहीं होता,

कभी इतना प्यार ही नहीं होता।

Mausam Agrawal

She is 22 year old girl from Nepal.She is currently pursuing C.A. and loves writing poems,shayaris and stories.Writing is her passion

.

Kami Hai Toh Bas Teri

Yaha sab hai
Phir bhi khali sa lagta hai
Tere na hone ka
Ahsas laga rehta hai

Tu itna dur hai mujhse
Ki baatein bhi nahi kar sakte
Milna toh tujhse abh bas khawab hi reh gaya
Tu mere karib tha sabse jyada
Tu hi sabse jyada dur ho gaya
Farz tujhe nibhana tha
Watan se jo tune kiya
Mera wadon ka hisab toh tune kiya hi nahi
Mana dur hum tab bhi the
Jab mahino mulakat na hoti thi

(2)

Par woh waqt bhi utna hi khaas tha
Khat ka jamana mano purana sa ho gaya ho
Par teri ek chitti se mujhe duniya bhar ki khusi mil jati thi
Aur teri kabhi kabhi ki gayi choti video call bhi
Nayi umeed de jati thi
Ladna bhi hota tha
Hum ruthte ,manate the
Par woh waqt abh kahan dubara aayega
Tere bin tanha sa mera hona
Abh tanha hi reh jayega

Alina Tamkanat

Hello friends
It's me Alina tamkanat
I like to see Dreams in an open eyes and then I like to work on them to fulfill it..
I'm passionate for facing camera for acting,modelling and for holding camera making new new videos and vlogs ..and I make my leg tired by traveling..
But my hobbies are to relaxing my eyes by reading some good books and moving my hand with my pen for writing some stories and shayiris
So, I work both of them. I follow my passion and work on my hobbies...
For improving my self and make better version of me.
Thank you....

Long Distance Love

When it hurts so bad, why does it feel so good? I wish this all made sense, I wish I understood. Not having you here with me is tearing me up inside, but I can't stop thinking about you no matter how hard I try. You know how I feel about you, and I know I want to spend the rest of my life with you, but it's so hard to do when I can't evenbe next to you. Why does it gotta be so complicated? Loving you feels so right, but at the same time, knowing I can't have you keeps me awake at night. I just want this to be simple, I just want you here with me, to look into your eyes, be held in your arms...then I'd truly be happy. Right now this distance between us is out of our control,but l'm still hoping one day soon, l'll get what l'm wishing for.....

Arijit Mondal

Arijit Mondal ,a boy with big dreams. He is very much hardworking and energetic guy and a reliable friend to hand around. He is a bookaholic in nature and loves to pen down his

feelings. He believes hardwork is the major key to success.

My First Love, Brother

Hey!You,yes You,listen;
You are my first companion,
in my first schooling.
And I am the first one to whom,
you share your love.
Whenever I get frustrated,
you motivate me,
With your own words.
When I go down to a wrong path,
you first dominate me,and
bring me in light.
And also I find your appreciation first whenever,
I do something great.
You are always on the verge,
of fulfilling my Wish.
Whatever problems appear,
you are trying to solve,
by yourself,so that it doesn't
affect my mind.
You are that person who,
teach me that,
inspiration comes from within.
Whenever I have problems,
I pray to God,and God sends You,
like a Cherub.
You are my best gift of God,
and You are the pillar of my life.
I want You forever.
God bless You.

Suhita S

Suhita, persuing her MA in English Literature, a Charming girl, who loves the magical spark of life on holding the air of positivism, her love for crazy fantasies never ends, she acts to make the most of every second by loving the simplest form of each individuals. She had been Co-author of 18+ anthologies under various publication and many more in progress. She is also a book reviewer. Her poems are published in the Magazine 'Artistic Athena' of June and July edition and in Digital Magazine 'Shelves Of Arts and Literature' Volume-1. She observes and feels everything by heart, spreading her colours all over. Her thoughts were soulfully penned!

(Instagram Handle @sparkling_wink)
(Mail Id: suhichutty171@gmail.com)

Is Ours A Long Distance Relationship?!

Though it means distance by kilometres
But I feel it by heart and mind
My drizzled air spinned and turned dry
Not separated but parted dimensional
Broken or Partially attached?
Pieces hit and it pains literally
Words tremble were silence masters
Will this end abruptly?!
Ample number of opportunities
Even though mistakes are repeated
Is my love taken for granted?
Think deep....
Is ours a long distance relationship?!

Saloni Lal Srivastava

She is Saloni Lal Srivastava daughter of Mr. Kumar Prashant and Mrs. Asha Sinha from Siwan, Bihar. She is a girl from a small town with her big dreams. Her life is all around her family, friends and career. In present she is purchasing B.sc in Botany hounors. She work as co author in 25+ anthologies. She is one of those who love to spread smile and positivity to everyone. Her instagram handle is @salonilalsrivastava.

रात हमसफर मेरी

रात हमसफर मेरी
यादों का दिया जलाती है
जब मेरा महबूब मुझसे रुका हो
तो रात हमसफर मेरी बन जाती हैं
जब कभी तनहाई में आंखें मेरी भर आए
यह रात उसकी सौगंध दिला
होठों पर मुस्कान ले आती है
जब कभी मेरा महबूब साथ ना हो
तो रात हमसफर मेरी बन जाती है

अधूरापन

ना जाने क्यों साथ होते हुए भी सबके
एक अधूरापन सा महसूस होता है
ना जाने क्यों इस दिल में
एक खालीपन सा लगता है
तेरी यादों के सहारे जी तो रहे हैं
पर तेरे बिन सब कुछ अधूरा सा लगता है...

Pragya Verma

Pragya Verma is born and raised in Prayagraj, Uttar Pradesh. She is currently pursuing Bachelor's in Computer Application. She is a poet and a writer. She also loves to make paintings and doing photography.

Distance Between Us

I'm missing our late night walks,
Sitting on roof and those deep talks.
Watching movies while eating pizzas,
Fighting for that last bite but sharing atlast.

Holding your hands tightly,
Felt like a flame burning brightly.
I'm crying, I'm crying for you,
This loneliness reminds me of you.

I wish you were here with me,
These scary nights scares me.
Nightmares don't go away,
And I couldn't find a way.

The distance between us is killing me,
And I just hope that time pass quickly.

दूरियों को भी सह लेंगे हम

दूरियों को भी सह लेंगे हम,
मगर यह साथ न छोड़ देना तुम।
हर पल रो कर भी इंतज़ार करेंगे हम,
बस किसी और के न होना तुम।

उन यादों को याद करके,
उन पलों में भी जी लेंगे हम,
कोई भी मजबूरियां आ जाएं,
तुम्हारा साथ न छोड़ेंगे हम।

वक्त हमेशा इंतहान लेता है,
उस इंतहान में सफल होंगे हम।
तुम साथ रहना ज़िंदगी भर,
हर मुश्किल से लड़ लेंगे हम।

प्यार किया है हमने, उसे निभाएंगे भी,
जो प्यार हमेशा न रहे, क्या वह प्यार है भी "?"

Akanksha Sinha

Akanksha Sinha is student by profession ,writer as passion. Lives in Patna,Bihar. She loves to portrait feelings by her poetry and quotes,she likes travelling and capturing moments. Heart healer by birth. She is co author of 15+ anthology. She loves to feel the nature. She is passionate &ambitious for her work.

Currently, she is been a co-author in several anthologies and compiling her first anthology named Zindagi-Ek-Ehsaas...

She has own page namely @merelabzz on Instagram.

लॉन्ग डिस्टेंस रिलेशनशिप

लॉन्ग डिस्टेंस वाला प्यार है अपना
तुझसे मिलने लगता है सपना
ख्वाबों में होती है रोज़ ही बाते
आओ कभी साथ बैठे के करे मुलाकाते
तरे पास होने का एहसास तो है
शपर तुम पास हो वो वाली बात नही
तुम्हारे साथ वक़्त बीतना अब सपना सा लगता है
तुम से दूर हो कर मुझे अपना सा लगता है

कॉल पे दूरियां कम सी लगती है
हर वक़्त आँखे नम सी लगती है
जब आती है याद तुम्हरी
करती हूँ मिलने की फरियाद हमारी
तेरे तस्वीर को सिने से लगा रखा है
तुझे कुछ इस तरह दिल में बसा के रखा है

लॉन्ग डिस्टेंस वाला प्यार है हमारा
वीडिओ कॉल बस अपना सहारा
तरे साथ लम्हा जीना चाहती हूँ
पकार हाथ तेरे चलना चाहती हूँ
मिलने का है वादा हमारा
साथ चलाना है इरादा हमारा

अनिल विश्वकर्मा

लेखक को श्री अनिल कुमार विश्वकर्मा के नाम से जाना जाता है, वे देश की राजधानी दिल्ली से सम्बन्ध रखते हैं। उनकी स्नातक की शिक्षा दिल्ली विश्वविद्यालय से हुई है तथा वर्तमान में वे एक प्रतिष्ठित संगठन में कार्यरत हैं। वे एक गम्भीर व ज़िम्मेदार युवक होने के साथ-साथ कर्तव्यनिष्ठ और पारिवारिक व्यक्ति भी हैं। अपने जीवन के दैनिक कार्यों में व्यस्त रहते हुए भी वे अपनी लेखन रुचि को जीवित रखते हैं। अपने स्नातकोत्तर के दौरान ही उनमें लेखन की रुचि उत्पन्न हो गई थी, किंतु इस कला को भौतिक स्वरूप देने में उन्हें कुछ समय लगा। उनके लेखन की प्रेरणा व स्रोत उनकी प्रिय जीवनसंगिनी है। वे थोड़े अल्पभाषी है किंतु कलम के माध्यम से वे अपनी बात कहना जानते हैं। वे अपनी रचनाओं और लेखनी के माध्यम से आप लोगों से जुड़ना चाहते हैं तथा साथ ही साथ यह भी कामना करते हैं कि आप लोगों का प्रोत्साहन व स्नेह भी उन्हें भरपूर मिले क्योंकि वे इस क्षेत्र में अभी नवीन हैं परंतु इस यात्रा में और आगे तक जाने की इच्छा रखते हैं।

मुकम्मल जहाँ।

तुझे पा लिया, तो लगता है कि,
एक मुकम्मल जहाँ मिल गया....,

मेरी ठहरी हुई दुनिया को,
एक नया कारवाँ मिल गया....,

मेरी ज़र्ज़र हो चुके हालात को,
एक नया आशियाँ मिल गया....,

मेरी दिल की बंज़र जमीन को,
एक बुंद का आसरा मिल गया....

,

गर तुम मेरे पास होती।

गर तुम मेरे पास होती,

हम हमेशा के लिये एक हो जाते,
एक दुसरे की आँखो में यूं ही खो जाते,
एक दुसरे की बाहों में सिमट जाते,
रोम-रोम में गुल खिल जाते,
ये चाहत कुछ ख़ास होती,
गर तुम मेरे पास होती।

सासों से सासें मिल जाती,
होठों से होठों की मुलाक़ात होती,
बैठ कर ढ़ेर सारी बात होती,
गर तुम मेरे पास होती।

इस रात की कोई सुबह न होती,
सारी दुरियां खत्म होती,
दो जिस्म एक जान होती,
गर तुम मेरे पास होती।

Mohua Chakraborty

An optimistic doer who sees the world with rose-coloured glasses and gets visible in the introvertly emitted spectra.

That Last Touch

Waking up in the cosy chair, caffeine running down the nerves,
Sleepless nights, piles of work, blobs of squirks,
Tincture of care I hardly could seek, until I had my 'superwoman' near.
Seven seas, fourteen countries away, 'she' sacrificed her desires for me to sway.
Her tears handcuffed my heart, it stays there and I bleed here each day..
Sensations of love & emotions are bagged for extrusion of my cardiomyocytes,
Haunts me that last touch cause it's been a quinquennial, my childhood fear to lose her smile.
Moments could shatter, I was far from my narrator.
The only gift was loneliness but longed for her caressing move, blessing my hairs,
And her lap that took to heaven, her admonishments on whatever done.
Tempted now to die on her feet, flying back to weaken my superwoman again.

The Letter Unmailed

It was in a while that I felt not to miss you anymore , not because I lost feelings but I realized you stay with me every second. Though I had been crying since you got consumed in work overseas and couldn't space up time for me but that's pretty fine, afterall I'm your most understanding panda who knows distance can't separate our hearts or articulation of heartbeats. I'm more focused on the fact that our contract of togetherness won't drown in the sea of career issues. Here I'm smiling with your memories and would mail you this only when you bring roses and my favorite chocolate box on my next birthday. Remember I'll love you more my teddy!

Sachin Banoudhiya

He is a student of Bsc
A Struggling Writter now Started Getting so many platforms
He Loves to do Audio Poetries & video Editing .
He's a Publish Co - author in so many Anthologies

Long Distance Bestfriendship

Finally Aahe gya Tha Wo Pal
After 729 Days Aakhir
Khudse Jo Milne Wala tha
Anjani Raaho se Lekr Jerry Tak Ka safar. .
Jo 2 Saal waste Kiye Uska Sabr.
6 Saalo Ki Duri Jo Mitani Thi .
Aakhir Meri Jerry Mere Paas Jo aani thi ..
Wo aagyi..
Baitha tha Akele Excitement Unpredictable thi saath. .
Jaise Tujhe Dekha
Dhadkane Kuch Pal Ke Liye Tham si Gyi . . .
Can't Believe
Jinu Mil he gyi ...
Wo Itni Pyaari hai
Uski Ibadat Karne Ki Chahat Hoti hai
Ye Dil machal sa jaata hai
Jab V uske kadmo ki aahat si Hoti hai
Kuch esa he hua Wo Meri Trf Jesi he badi puri duniya meri
Liye Tham Si gyi
Kisi Shayar Ke Alfaazo Ki Tarh
Bs Chalti aarhi thi .
Ruki To ek Pal ke liye Jese Jahan ruk gya.
Mere Face Ki smile Jese
Uchl Uchl kr keh Rhi Ho

To Yehi Hai Hamare Aane Ki Wajh. .

Shresth Bhargava (Yash)

Shresth Bhargava (Yash), is an emerging writer,author as well as compiler from The city of Love, The city of Taj AGRA.In his point of view , 'we can bring positive changes in the lives of peoples as well as we can ir-radicate social-evil's from our community by the help of our writings'.Apart from his writtings ,he is also a CA Aspirant ,His aim of life is to help mankind and bring positive changes in the lives of his countrymen .He has won various certificates in various competitions,He is always there for help of peoples in need .He is nature loving person,He is a devotee of Lord Shiva .He respect the ones who respects him and himself .He is verey friendly person,for him his family and friends is his lifeline
Intagram ID @yashbhargava2000

मेरा प्यार

मैं आपको अपने विचारों और सपनों में देखता हूं,
जब मैं जागता हूं तो कितना वास्तविक लगता है।
आप मुझे आराम देने के लिए यहाँ नहीं हैं,
लेकिन जल्द ही मुझे उम्मीद है कि आप होंगे।
कोई भी वास्तव में जानता या समझता नहीं है;
तुम्हारे हाथों में मेरा दिल है।
मेरा प्यार वही है जो आप वास्तव में खुद के हैं।
जल्दी आओ और हमारे घर को एक घर बनाओ।

उन दीवारों के अंदर आप अपना समय कर रहे हैं,
यहाँ मेरे साथ नहीं होना तुम्हारा एकमात्र सच्चा अपराध है।
आपके जीवन में अन्य लोग आएंगे और जाएंगे,
लेकिन मेरा प्यार सच्चा है, और मुझे यकीन है कि आप जानते हैं

मैं धनी नहीं हो सकता या सबसे प्रिय व्यक्ति,
लेकिन मैं तुमसे बहुत प्यार करता हूँ; आप मेरे सूर्य हो।
आप हर बार फोन करने पर मेरे जीवन पर प्रकाश डालते हैं।
जब समय समाप्त हो जाता है, तो मैं गिरना शुरू कर देता हूं।
तुम मेरे सितारे हो, तुम मेरे चाँद हो,
आपके साथ होने से बहुत जल्द आ जाएगा।
इसलिए जब आप सोते हैं, तो इसे दिल पर ले लें,
कोई भी या कुछ भी हमें अलग नहीं रखेगा।

Meenakshi Sharma

Hi, she is Meenakshi sharma , a 19 years old girl dreaming to be a writer someday, she believes that nothing is powerful than words so she tries her best to change the word for a good sake. "Insta id - minepoetry_

Ye Dooriyan

Khte hai dooriyan ishq ko aur badha deti hai,
Soye hue jazbaato ko bhi kya khoob jaga deti hai ,
Dil ki gehrayi mein chahat ki boondein barsha deti hai,
Toh kuch iss tarah,
Kuch iss tarah hme apne rango mein bde masoomiyat se bhiga deti hai !

Ek call ke intezaar mein aankhe nam kra deti hai,
Toh aawaz sunte hi ek sukoon ki hawa daur jaati hai,
Paas na hote hue bhi har ek lmhe teri maujoodgi ka ilm krati hai,
Sach hi toh hai,
Dooriyan ishq ko aur badha jaati hai !

Mansi Kanungo

मेरा नाम मानसी कानूनगो है, मैं इंदौर (मध्यप्रदेश) से हूं। मैं 19 वर्ष की हूं , लिखना मेरा पेशा नहीं मेरी आदत है।

(1)

तनहा है तु, तनहा हु मैं
जितनी है दूर तु, उतना ही दूर हूं मैं,
साथ आ नहीं सकते हम चाह कर भी क्योंकि,
जितनी मजबूर हैं तु, उतना ही मजबूर हूं मैं...।।

(2)

अब तो ना कोई खबर है उनकी,और ना ही कोई पता है
दूर हो गये है एक दूसरे से, शायद यही अब हमारी सज़ा है...
बस थोड़े से हम खफा हैं, और ना जाने उनकी क्या वजह है,
पर इन दूरियों में भी एक अलग ही मज़ा है.....।

(3)

कुछ किस्से दफन हैं ज़हन में तेरे उसे दफ़न ही रहने दो
के कुछ हिस्से कफ़न बनें है जिंदगी में मेरे उसे कफ़न ही रहने दो!!

Parwana Bibi

Parwana Bibi a little moody and shy girl .She want to see people happy and she is so cute .And she is very talented and never give up any situation .Let's see what she write for us.

(1)

Har waqt khayalon mein rehete ho ,
Har raat sapne mein aate ho ,

Tum wahan aur mein yahan bas tanha tanha din gujarte hain
Bas ab aur duri sahi nahi jati ab to aakar gale se lagalo humein ...

(2)

Mera dil tere pyar ke bina adhura thha ,
Tumne isse apne pyar se saja kar ghar banaya thha .....
Lekin iss duri ki majal to dekho hum ko juda karne chali hai ,
Per usko yeh nahi pata hum jab tak ek dusre ko samajhenge tab tak koi bhi humein juda nahi kar sakta hai .....

Muskan Gupta

She is Muskan Gupta ,lives in Ayodhya Uttar Pradesh. She is 20 years old.

She is a writer by heart.

She is doing graduation from Delhi University. She have a burning desire to achieve her aim . She want to explore in the field of writing.

She writes to express not to impress.

She writes her quote on myquoteapp app:- https://www.yourquote.in/cutipie_muskan

On Instagram- mukhtalif90

(1)

Aaj bhi kuch badla nahi
Tumhare door jaane se yaha aaj bhi kuch badla nahi ,badli hai toh sirf meri aadatein, meri ibaadatein....
Tumhare door jaane se yaha aaj bhi kuch badla nahi ...
Tumhare door chale jaane se aaj bhi teri yaadein mere dilon mein taaza hai, kuch in saalon mein badla hai toh sirf tere judaa hone ka woh dardnaak ehsaas..
Tumhare door jaane se yaha aaj bhi kuch badla nahi ...

(2)

Uski Raah
Uski raah tak ke mujhe barso ho gaye... Lekin imtihaan ki ghari aaj tak barkaraar hai...
Ab sadiyaan bhi guzar jaaey toh kya ... ussey juri har guftgu ka khayal toh aaj tak hai...
Uski har arzoo ko khuda bhi kabool kar le kuch aise uske alfaaz hai..
Har shikassth mein sbko maat de kuch aise uske andaaz hai...

(3)

यु तो !!!

यु तो! उनकी आखें रोई होगी... हमारे जाने पर ...

यु तो ! हमसे मिलने की कोशिशे की होगी ... हमारे मुँह फेरने पर ...

यु तो! तकदीरे बदली होगी ..हमारे चले जाने पर...

यु तो! फ़रियाद की होगी ...हमारे ना मिलने पर ...

यु तो! सांसें थमी होगी ... हमारे जनाज़े को दफन करते वक़्त ...

Hynul Jaseena

This is Miss. Hynul Jaseena.
She is a teacher by profession and a resident of Mysore, Karnataka.
She loves to read and write.
Her passion of becoming a writer is still a blazing fire.
She has written many thoughts and quotes on life.
Do follow her official Instagram page @binte_sadakath for more such quotes

Mysore to Hyderabad

Our souls were apart,
But hearts weren't.
You may be far off the place,
But never from my heart's solace.
I wish to see you once,
And dream gives a glance.
Dreams are beautiful than revery,
Atleast then my heart gets a recovery.
My heart yearns to hold you tight,
This is known only to the silent night.
Remember, you're engraved in my heart,
There can be no ways to get apart.
Our souls unites one day for sure,
And let the world admire us and adore.

पुलिन भारती

ये पुलिन भारती हैं। जो पेशे से सिविल इंजीनियर हैं पर दिल से एक कवि। जन्म तो पटना,बिहार में हुआ लेकिन बड़े हुए पंचग्राम, असम में।

इनकी लिखने की कला अपने आप में एक अलग पहचान है जो कई विषयों पर है।

अभी तक इनकी कविताएं इनकी डायरी तक ही सीमित थी अब ये उन(कविताओं) को दुनिया से परिचय करवा रहे हैं।

आप इनकी प्रेरक विचारों को इनके इंस्टाग्राम @bharti_pulin पर भी पढ़ सकते हैं।

दिल का रिश्ता

दर्द के इस जहाँ में रिश्ता एक सपना सा,
इस भरी हुई गैरों की दुनिया में है कोई अपना सा।
तकलीफ होती है जब उसे तो अनचाहे दर्द होता है मुझे,
पर अक्सर ही मुस्कुराते हुए बहुत याद आती है वो मुझे।

कई दफा तो ये समझ नही आता,
क्यों होती तकलीफ उसे तो आंसू मेरी आँखों से निकल जाता?
क्या कहीं प्यार तो नहीं है उसके लिए,
फिर सोचता हूँ क्या प्यार होना ज़रूरी है उसके साथ के लिए?

पल-पल जाने-अनजाने उसकी बातें मुझे याद आती हैं,
और पल ही पल उसकी मुस्कुराहट के साथ उसकी हसीं भी मुझ में समा जाती है।
अक्सर ही याद करता हूँ उसके चेहरे का वो नूर जब वो मुस्कुराती है,
फिर समझ जाता हूँ कि ये मुस्कुराहट है उसकी जब-जब उसे मेरी याद आती है।

दूरी

मैंने देखा है तड़पते हुए लोगों को,
बिन मोहब्बत अधुरों को,
कोई किसी से दूर रह कर भी सच्चे प्यार में है,
तो कई किसी के साथ हो कर भी तन्हा हैं।

इश्क़ तो हर इंसान करता है,
पर ज़रूरी ये है कि को किसके लिए तड़पता है।
कई बार लोग खामोश रह कर भी इकरार करते हैं,
और कई बार शोर मचा कर इनकार भी करते हैं।

अपनी दिल की सुनो और कह दो जिससे तुम मोहब्बत करते हो,
क्या पता वो इंसान भी आपके इशारे के इंतज़ार में हो,
कभी-कभी खामोशी भी दिल टूटने की वजह बनती है,
पर अगर सच्चे दिल से की हुई मोहब्बत हो तो वही एक-दुसरे की
खुशी होती है।

Puja Kundu

Mbbs student, Budding author.

नज़दीकिया

हालत मेरा हो ना हो, में हर हाल में तेरा हूँ,
हाथ तेरा हो ना हो, में हर साथ में तेरा हूँ,
दूरियाँ चाहे जीतनी भी हो, हमेंशा तेरे आस पास हूँ,
लफ़्ज़ तेरा हो ना हो,
मेरे हर एक अल्फाज बस तुझ पर खतम होती हैं,
रास्ता तेरा हो ना हो,
मैं हर एक मोड़ पे तेरे इंतज़ार में हूँ,
मंज़िल तेरा हो ना हो,
मैं हर राह में, बन मुसाफिर तेरा हूँ,
दर्द चाहें जितनी भी हो, दवा-ए- इश्क़ का इलाज़ हूँ,
किस्सा तेरा हो ना हो,
हजारो किस्सो के साब् हिस्सों में भी में बस तेरा ही हूँ।

Shobha Rajpal

Shobha Rajpal is writer by passion. Her love for hindi is divine. She feels quite comfortable with hindi rather english as she loves her mother tongue. She is Hindi graduated and teacher by profession.

तेरे बिन तन्हा यहां :

मैं तेरे बिन तन्हा यहां
तू मेरे बिन तन्हा वहां
तू है बेचैन वहां
मैं भी बेचैन यहां
राते भी खामोश मेरी
हसरते भी खामोश मेरी
सांसो मैं है शोर सरगम भी खामोश है
ना राज खोलू मैं,आके मुझको संभाल लेना
आ जाओ कुछ पल चाहे मुहब्बत ना करना
क्योंकि जख्मी दिल रह गया
तेरे बिन तन्हा यहां

Priyanshi Kamboj

Priyanshi kamboj is a student of Delhi and she thinks that poetry and words complete a person . And we should always express ourselves like she is and her writings has lead to many achievements in her life

.

Caress: Myth Or Reality

I am thinking since a week that how it's all gonna be when the dark days will past us and we will merrymake that moment by taking out masks like wedding bouquet has been thrown by the bride. When we will be unshackled out of the handcuffs. Oh that feeling and I can bet that we all faced dicey situations about should we go out to meet our loved ones or stay home to save our lives for those loved ones . Humans such a character that ought to do something totally opposite to what's been told to do because following implications would be so boring . Nowadays it's not more than a thriller movie , we are living but it's not clear that whether there's going to be a happy ending or not . Lockdown has taught us many things , Firstly that we need the touch of a person we love just like we need air to breathe . Secondly how productive we all can be . Start exploring the area in which you can do impeccable . Time can fly and will be out just like time bomb . Missing friends and family , sitting miles away from them and thinking that if we knew any of it would be happening then we would have hugged each other tighter and have seen each other more , could have taken out time more out of our chores to do. Now we all could only wonder what it would be to melt into someone's sweet arms and stay there for eternity. Touch is soft like feather it's myth or reality . We all are living five feets apart in real now.

Anisha Panda

She is a cute little girl full of joy and respect. A little complicated. Hard to understand. But if you once get to know her you can see how wonderful she is really. She is one of my best friend Anisha Panda.

फौजी का प्यार

बारिश की बूंदें तेरी यादें लायी हैं ,
जुदाई की रात अपने साथ लायी है ॥

एक बार फिर तड़पना होगा मुझे ,
मुझे फिर छोड़ के जाना होगा तुझे ॥

किस्मत का खेल तोह देखो , रोक भी नहीं सकती तुम्हे ;
चाहे पल पल मरती रहूं तेरी यादों में ,
फिर भी दामन से बांध नहीं सकती तुम्हे ॥

देश से प्यार है मुझे भी ,
देश से प्यार है तुझे भी ,
मेरा प्यार तो बस घर तक है ,
तेरा जूनून तोह बस सरहद है ॥

फिर लौट के आओगे यह वादा कर के जाना ,
सरहद पे जा के हमें तुम भूल न जाना ॥

Smriti Kumari

Smriti kumari is student by profession,writer by passion.she lives in Delhi,India. She is 2nd year student, pursuing bsc(h) maths from Rajdhani college,Delhi University. She is very passionate, inquisitive and hardworking for her work.she is also part of many anthologies.The pen is a strong weapon for her to portray her feelings.let's enjoy her writing and shower your love and support..

तन्हा इश्क़

दर्द-ए-घूंट पिया नहीं जाता,
तेरे बिन कहीं जिया नहीं जाता।
तू सब्र है मेरा,तू मेरी सांस है,
तू है तो ज़िन्दगी गुलज़ार है।
तेरे बिन नहीं चैन कहीं,
हर तरफ़ तन्हाई है।
दिल की पुकार में तुम,
तू ही मेरी परछाई है।
ख्वाबों में बसे हो तुम,
तुझमें मैनें सुकून पायी है।
तेरे दूर जाने पर,
पागल सी खुद को पाई हूं।
बस अब!
दर्द-ए-घूंट पिया नहीं जाता,
तेरे बिन कहीं जिया नहीं जाता।

Dwiza

This Is Dwiza Daughter of Mr. Pardeep Kalra And Mrs. Devinder Writing Is Never Made to Do, It Just Happens. I Never Had Any Inspiration of Writing. My Inner Feelings Made Me This Capable. I Wish to Write Further and Get A Name For Myself By This Passion Of Mine.

You Can Visit Her Online on Instagram

@Silhouette__Emotions

कोई पूछे मुझसे मतलब इश्क़ का

मैं तुम्हारा नाम बतादूँगी
कोई पूछे मासूमियत क्या होती हैं
मैं तुम्हारा चहरा दिखादूँगी
कोई पूछे पागलपन क्या हैं
मैं तुम्हें देखकर मुस्कुरादूँगी
कोई पूछे ख़्वाब कैसे होते हैं
मैं आँखों मे अपनी तेरी सूरत दिखादूँगी
कोई पूछे खूबसूरती का मतलब
मैं उसे तुम्हारी आंखे दिखादूँगी
कोई पूछे भरोसा क्या हैं
मैं उसे तुम्हारा पता बतादूँगी
इश्क़ में हृदों की बात करने वालो को
मैं अपनी कहानी सुनादूँगी
कोई पूछे मुझसे सुकून का मतलब
मैं तुम्हें गले से लगालूंगी।।

(2)

बड़ी भीड़ दिखती हैं इस दुनिया में,
पर अपनो का कोई बसेरा ना दिखा,
नजरें गयी जहाँ तक कोई मेरा ना दिखा,
एक मिराज सा बन रह गया अपनो का प्यार,
जो भी मिला बस खुदगर्जी से मिला,
इन लाखों की भीड़ में कोई अपना तराना ना मिला ।
मैं भटकती रही अपनो के प्यार के लिये,
इस प्यास को बुझा दे एसा दरिया ना मिला,
बहुत रोयी मैं अकेली बैठ के....
पर आसूँ किस में समाये,इन्हे कोई किनारा ना मिला

Shweta Rajput

Shweta rajput, she is from from motihari bihar has pretty and beautiful personality girl which can be called a perfect person

She is a graduate girl with small experience in private service sector.
She is an emerging writer and dream to achieve something in the field of writing. she got great support from superstar friend and now she isinteroduced to write in anthology book
She has passion for dancing and writing

(1)

Tere bin tanha yaha..
Najaane ye dil kyu khoya khoya sa rhta hai

Kisse kahu ki
har pal mera suna suna sa rehta hai.
Jisse kabhi mohbatt hui thi siddto wali..
Wo ab mujhse rutha rutha sa rehta hai

Din to kaisi bhi kat jati
Raton ko teri yadein dhoodhla dhoodhla sa rahta hai

Sacha kahu bichhad kr tujhse
Mujhe sab tanha tanha sa lgta hai

Hamaari adhuri kahaani ab khwaab ban gyi hai
Tere bin tanha yaha jaise sanse dum todti..
Zindgani likhi gai hai.
Ab ye ankhi kahani v apna apna sa lgta hai..

Sach kahu tere jaane ke baad
Ye shamaa bhi tanha tanha sa lgta hai

Avi Srivastava

He is an engineering student aimed to make his name in computer world.... Poetry is not only is his hobby but also a way to express his feelings....

साथ हमारा.....

हसीन लम्हो का पिटारा था वो साथ हमारा....
वो नाव की सवारी और अस्सी घाट का किनारा....
वो छिप के मिलना और गोलगप्पो पे गुजारा....
तुम न हो साथ मेरे बस इन यादों का हैं सहारा....

बदला था मैंने शहर बस, जज़्बात मेरे आज भी वहीं हैं....
चाहे छोड़ चुकी हैं साथ मेरा, फिर भी वो मुझमें बाकी कहीं हैं....
दूरी की वजह से थोड़ा, नही दे पाया उसे मैं वक्त....
अब बिन उसके जियूँ या बहा लूँ अपना रक्त..

.

ये दूरी बीच हमारे.....

माना दूरी बहुत हैं बीच हमारे, पर प्यार हमारा बट नही सकता....
सीने में हैं ये दिल मेरा, आज भी तुमहारे लिए हैं धड़कता...
हाथो में हाथ लिए नही घूम सकते, पर रोज वीडियो कॉल पर कर सकते हैं बातें....
आंखों में आंखे डाले, जाहिर कर सकते हैं अपनी जज़्बातेँ....

हो सकता हैं आ जाए, कभी-कभी रिश्तों में कड़वाहट....
शक के घेरो में फस कर, करने लग जाये एक दूसरे से शिकायत....
कर लेंगे हम लड़ाईयां थोड़ी, हो जयगा मन हल्का...
शान्त मन से फिर हमलोग, साथ निभायँगे एक-दूजे का....

Hida Naz

Little writer

Tere Bin Tanha Yaha:-

Ek Muddat se aarzoo hai ki,
Mile tumse tumhare hokar....
Gazab kuchh yu huva ki ham
Rahe hi na hamare hokar..
Gumsum Sa hai Manzar Dil ka
Ki tum aao to ye Abad ho jaaye...
Tere bin tanha yahan
Ke dekho kahin Ham,
uhi khaak Na Ho jaaye....
Ki aao, dekho kahin waqt barbad Na Ho jaaye
Batane the Jo tumko Dil ke Raaz....
Wo raaz kahin Raaz hi Na rah jaaye
izhaar, iqrar najane kya kya baki hai abi..
Tum pass nahi to kya tumhari yaad bhi kafi hai abhi!!
Tere bin tanha yaha:-

Komal Surwade

Mr. Komal Surwade, born on 20 February 1999 in Maharashtra, currently settled in Nashik, Engineering Student (CIVIL). Writing is one of my hobbies.

An Engineer, Story writer, poet, Dancer.

I love reading novel's.

I'm a Potterhead.

I love K-pop (BTS is my favourite).

I love watching Korean drama too.

I Worked as co-author in some anthologies like "Black", "College Romance", "Life Sahi Hai".

I've had to accept that everyone cannot

love me. Because when there's love, there's hate. When there's light, there's dark.

"A letter from her"

Dear Darling,

Long-distance relationships are hard. And no one else quite realizes. There are more reasons to fight, to cry, to break up. But distance also gives us a reason to love harder, what any other couple needs. To fight harder, because, in the end, we have something to gain. Living apart from you is more difficult than I imagined. I see reminders of you everywhere I look, & they make me ache to be near you again. No matter what I do or say, I just can't stop thinking about you. It's sweet torture to know that we are physically apart and at the same time so close to each other because our hearts beat as one.

Today, as I was drinking my coffee, I was recollecting some of our past moments together. I remember our first walk together when you took my hand & hold it till we got back. Every day spent with you is a day full of blessings. Whenever I feel sad all that I'll ever need is you and your smile because that is my biggest happiness and blessing.

You want to know how much I appreciate your every gesture and how much you look forward to being like me. My love for you has increased further in this lockdown.
Thank you for loving me.

Your_Dear_Girl

Lokesh Upadhyay

Lokesh Upadhyay, resident of buxar district in Bihar, presently he is a student in class 12th Dandi Swami sahajanand saint Vinova college. He has a keen interest in writing his heart out in the form of small poems, porses and verses. He hope you will enjoy reading his work and appreciate it.
Thank you..

मै गलत, तू सही!!!

माना कि कुछ गलतियां हुई है हम से किसी जमाने में,
कुछ अनजाने में तो कुछ दुनिया को दिखाने में,
लेकिन उसमें भागीदार तू भी तो था,
माना उन गलतियों का शाया आज भी हमारा पीछा नहीं छोड़ता ,
दिन में बेच्येनी देता,और रातों मै रुलाता है,
जानते हो कई सवालों का बवंडर आज भी मुझे सताता है,
काश उस दिन मै खुद पर काबू कर पता,
काश मै तुझे बचाने के लिए,
उस दिन एसा न किया होता,
इस बात का अहेसास रह रह के मुझे डरती है,
उस चीज का आज भी मुझे ग्लानी है,
और तेरी गलती मुझे भूलानी है,
हालात एक दिन सुधरेंगे इस बात का मन में आश है ,
मुझे नहीं तुम से दूर जाना है,
जो हम ने खोया है ,
उसको एक दिन पाना है,
फिर से तुझे अपना बनाना है,
मेरे दिल से मेरा सुकून छीन गया,
मेरे जीने का वजूद छीन गया,
अब बस किसी से भी दिल लगने की कोशिश करता हूं ,
लेकिन लगता है कि मेरे सीने से मेरा दिल ही छीन गया।

मैं गद्दार, तुम वफादार!!!

खुद को बफादार बताने वाले ,
मुझे सबके सामने बेवफ़ा जताने वाले,
एक बार खुद को एहसाह दिलाओ,
तुम किस किस से और कितना सच्चा प्यार किए हो मुझे बताओ।
सबसे चिकनी चुपड़ी बातें कर ,
सबका दिल लुभाते हो,
उन्हीं के पीठ पीछे ,उनके मजे उठाते हो।
दस - दस लड़कियों से बात कर के खुद को ईमानदार बताते हो,
एक लड़की के चक्रव्यूह में फस के अपने दोस्त को गालीया सुनाते हो,
अपने बातों के आगे किसी को कुछ न लगाते हो,
अरे जाओ जाओ इतना कुछ करने के बाद भी तुम खुद को बफादार बताते हो,
बेशर्मी का सरा हद्द पार कर के आते हो,
किसी को भी बाबू सोना बोल के अपना बनाते हो,
बाद में उसको छोड़ के किसी नए के साथ मौज मनाते हो,
क्या यही तुम खुद को ईमानदार बताते हो,
चलो चलो निकलो आए बड़े,
मुझे गद्दार, और खुद को वफादार बताने वाले

Raghav Laximan Gawde

His name is Raghav laximan Gawde as he resident from Pale Bicholim Goa.As he graduated from government polytechnic bicholim college.Love to write articles poems quotes.Formally he is Engineer in profession and poet as well as literature in passion.

Long distance life
(Away from family)

Long distance life
Is very difficult
Because the people
who live away from
Their close once
Feel the pain of
Separation from
Their loved once

Long distance life
In which they can't
Get family atmosphere
As they want to adjust
Their life with situation

In long distance life
They have to sacrifice
Their needs and
And had to live their
Life with what they have

Aditya Srivastava

Aditya is a future engineer. He had also been part a of 10+ anthologies and writes when he desires to.He wants to make his career in research field and wants to find something great for the good cause of the world.

You can connect to him at: @b.e.z.u.b.a.n__d.i.l

Jeene Ko Majboor

Na jane kyu tere bin
Tanha reh nahi pata hai
Mera dimaag tujhe sochne ko
Majboor kar deta hai
Or ek taraf teri yaadein hai
Jo saalo se jurne ki kosis me hai
Kambakhat phir se us dil ko
Chur chur kar deta hai
Par kar bhi kya sakte hai
Ki tu to chor ke chali gai tanha
Par ek teri yaadein hi to hai
Jo ghut ghut ke hi sahi
Magar fir se jeene ko
Majboor kar deta hai.

Maitreyee

She is Maitreyee. Don't go by her age since she can bemuse you with her words. She is bubbly, scintilating and ambitious! She has an expertise in story telling, micro tales while also weaving words into beautiful poetries. She is a foodie and loves cooking too.

An Open Letter

To,
someone who keeps coming to my mind no matter what time of the day it is,

How can you be so cruel, so heartless, so ruthless..! Do you even realise how many days and nights have i spent thinking about you, and more than that ' us' ? Thinking while embracing the adorable pink teddy you gifted me on my birthday, thinking while staring at the magnificent ring you put on my sleek, well manicured finger and recalling how i was blushing at that moment, thinking while looking at myself in the mirror after putting on that pulchritudinous black gown for which you complimented me and also couldn't help yourself but just kept gawking at me in the party, and while imagining all this in my head i reimagine all those precious moments of you embracing me gently in your arms while caressing my long black hair and i, thanking god for endowing me with the best gift of my life, YOU!! But suddenly everything seems to evanesce and as i get up, coming out of my fantasies, I realise that you are nowhere to be found apart from my wretched heart and oblivious mind. You are not here with me but just within me!
But you know what tonight it is more about missing you, than it has ever been about loving you. Meet me soon..!

.

With love
From,
Someone who counts each passing day and just wishes to catch a sight of you with her!

Adarsh Kumar Priyadarshi

Adarsh Kumar Priyadarshi is a school going boy form a small town called Hajipur, Bihar. His father servers the nation in Indian Army. And his mother is a housemarker. He is co-author of 40+ anthology . As he is proud to be the son of a loyal army man so he too wants to do something great for his mother-land. As he has a great zeal in medical field so he is currently even struggling with his journey to reach his destination, his goal i.e. to be a renowned doctor. He always thanks his parents, teachers, friend and God for what he is now.

His debut, book will be launched soon.

You can follow him on Instagram (@adarsh_priyadarshi_03)

(1)

You came into my life
like shelter from the storm,
your magic keeps my spirits high...
and your love keeps me warm.
No matter how far you are but
It doesn't affect our condition.

(2)

Nither her husband
Nor she is his wife
He is her everything
This is true love
It's not mean u merry her
It's all about is she
Happy or not in her life.

Sanjida Khan

Sanjida is a student at Vidhaan Public School..She likes to write and sketch

(1)

Ye khaani hai ek ldkii or uski bua ki...aanya 5th standard mein aayi thi ek din jab vo schl se ghar vapas lautii to usne dekha ke uski mummy ghar nhi hai usne apni bua se pucha bua mom kha hai? bua ne kha beta vo yha se alag chle gye hai agra...,agra me rhnge aapke mummy papa ab se us din aanya bht udaas thi vo soch rhi thi ke uske parents se itna doir kese rhegi vo ..pr us din se uski bua ne uska khyaal rkha kabhi bhi use kisi ki kami mehsoos nhi hone di.

(2)

Kuch saalo baad uske parents wapas aaye or use apne saath lejane ke liye kha pr aanya nhi maani kyuki vo apni bua se ab 2 pal ke liye bhi alag nhi reh skti thi..pr bua ne use smjhaya ke aanya dekho ye tumhare parnets hai tumhe jana pdega hmsha apne parents ki baat maan na..bua ki baat maan kr aanya chali gyi...fir kuch time baad uske parents foreign me rhne lge pr aanya hnesha apni bua ko yaad krti thi use aaj bhi apni bua ke saath vo dost wala rishta yaad tha raato baatein krna yaad tha...ye doriya uske or uski bua ke beech hmesha uski aankhe nam kr diya krti thi...pr fir bhi is long distance ne kabhi bhi aanya ke mann me uski bua ke kiye pyaar kam nhi kiyaa...Hmesha sochti thi ki bua se mil paaye kyuki is duri me tanhaiyaa bht thi...

.

Vanshika Gupta

Vanshika Gupta, born and raised in India; 17 years old now. Coming to her goals and career, she don't have any short time goal. All she wants to be is a writer. She wants her words to be the reason behind her success. Had been writing since past 4 years, and would want to carry this occupation forever.

(1)

Dear broken heart,
How do you mend?
I tend to be fine and you pretend
Umm ya okay, being my friend?
.
Its another day
come on heal yourself,
Free me away someday
please for God sake!
.
Why did I choose you
over my mind;
If you were kind
or me being blind?
.
I'm drunk,
You're my poison,
Get em out of this confusion
Tell that was a wrong decision;
.
My heart you're my song
Hell again, make me strong,
Huh, it's hurtin' bad
Will you still not mend?
.
My unhappy soul
Until when will you pretend,
Dear broken heart,
Will you still not mend?
Will you still not mend?

Nelofer Talukdar

Born in 2000, Nelofer Talukdar is a B.A 1st semester student-assistant teacher. She has immense faith in God and believes that He is always with her in every walk of life. She constantly strives to achieve the best out of everything. She is very fond of arts, crafts and writing. Her biggest dream is to be the reason behind bringing a bright and everlasting smile her father's face. She aspires to become a defence officer in the near future and work for her mother land.

Long Distance

Long distance relationship is always true.
True love exists and it can be found,
In the most unexpected places.
It makes us to become a better person,
By teaching us the value of patience.
A long distance relationship will help us to discover our partners true intentions.
Absence makes the heart grow fonder.
Distance is not for the fearful,
It's for the "bold".
Distance unites where we miss,
Beats of two hearts.
And at last we should,
Believe in the immeasurable;
Power of Love.

Saloni Santosh Gawas

She is from Goa.
She is a Science student who completed her 12th std this year.
She has taken a step forward for her 1st year of undergraduate course.
She is passionate about writing since she was in 6th std.
She is a night sky viewer and loves to write about stars.
As writing is a passion which is quite rare and sometimes left unnoticed, she got great support from her friends. And now she is introduced to write in anthology books
.

Those Meetings Are Special

The Drawer full of useless things..
Carries memories
Worth as precious pearls..

Standing on the terrace under the night sky I was thinking about you. The way I was feeling the wind it's like having you beside. Those twinkling stars assuming like your words, your silly jokes.

We don't meet frequently, and even someday we met by chance we can't talk the way we want, it's just a smile that makes my whole day.
Really, Is this way two best friends are?
Maybe not.
And that's the beauty of our bond. Even when we know we are not gonna meet for months there is not even a slightest change in the bond we share.
After months there comes a day actually 'Our Day'. Our dayout, when there is non-stop talks. That happiness is just amazing and that compensate for all the days we urge for a meet.

The most special thing that keep us connected are those things which we exchange during our meet.
Those letters, small gifts and even those chocolate rappers which I keep safe as our memories.

Best friend is someone who scolds you for your mistakes, beats you for no reason, pampers you when you feel low. Their one hug is like your all problems are vanished.
Meetings become special when the person is special.

Reshmi Vernekar

Reshmi Maheshwar vernekar has completed her Master degree in (hindi language) and currently doing bechular degree in education (b.ed) at pragati women's collge of education at torxem she want to become a teacher her hobbies are reading books,cooking, she also like to do social services

(1)

तू पास होकर भी मेरे पास नहीं

दूर रहकर भी एक दुजे के दिल मे रहते है। दूरियों से फर्क नही पड़ता बात तो दिल की नजदीकियों की होती है। तेरी एक मुस्कुराहट नया जीवन सा देती है।

मै तुम्हारे पास न होकर भी पास हूँ। तू पास होकर भी मेरे पास नहीं। हर दिन रात तुम्हारे बारे में सोचती रहती हूँ। हर किसी में तुझे ढूंढती हूँ। तुम्हारी हर पल हर घड़ी याद आती है। तुम्हारे कॉल का इंतजार करती हूं; तुम मेरे दिमाग में हर रोज आते हो, तुम्हारे जो वादे, तुम्हारी हर रोज की बातें, तुम्हारा जो किसी बात का रूठ जाना याद आता है। तुम्हारा जो मुझ पर बिना मतलब का रुठना, कहा गया वह वक्त जो सिर्फ हम दोनो का था?

ये दूरियाँ कैसी है, ये मजबूरियाँ कैसी है? तुमसे दूर रहकर भी ये मोहब्बत बढ़ती जा रही है। कैसे और किससे कहूं की तुम्हारी बहुत याद आती है। तुम्हारा जो मेरा हर दिन खयाल रखना, कहाँ हो, क्या कर रही हो, वहाँ क्यों गयी, नही जाना वहाँ सब बातें याद आती है। कहाँ गया वह तुम्हारा मुझे मनाना? यह सब बहुत याद आता है। हो सके तो वापस आ जाना क्यों की तू पास होकर भी मेरे पास नहीं।

Vaishnavi Naik

She is a girl with grace and simplicity. She is currently pursuing her bachelors in science in zoology from Dhempe college of arts and science in Goa. She is a sky gazer, a singer by interest, passionate photographer and a super complex person. She likes to travel and loves the smell of mountain air. She likes to make friendship with unknown people. She is a proud NCC cadet and loves INDIA

Long-Distance Relationship With Our Own Self.

Incarcerated in this outer physical world, we all beautifully fail to recognise our own self. Only some sharp-witted souls are successful in achieving their inner peace with a strong amount of bond with their own self. We are so engaged in thinking about our life and future time that we are unable to lend some time to our own self. Although the soul dwells within us, still we encounter this long-distance connection with it.

I asked a random individual...

We serve perfect regrets over it but never try to unravel the cause of it. Who we are, what we do, what we think and how we see is all because of this inner spiritual body which guides us and provides us with every possibility. We should embrace the beauty of our soul. We should focus once in a day on self-growth. We must pay respect to this eternal beauty.

That one day when all of us will be successful in providing some time to our own self, we all will attain peace and the whole human race shall thereby live in harmony.

Payal Singhal

Payal Singhal, a commerce graduate. She is a bibliophile who believes that there is magic in writing, which gives her the liberty to express herself, and most importantly, given the privilege to become soliloquy. She writes to bring a positive impact on society, and she knew pen and paper never judge but give a solution and peace every time.

Both Are Distant.

I keep falling for him and the moon.
Both are distant. I don't know it's a curse or boon.

I speak to both. One can't reply, one does not.
Still, I love them. The mind asks why, but the heart says why not.

I see Moon glimmer and his glittering eyes,
Then telling them less than wine is unwise.

I decided not to love, to both of them.
Then I look at the sky and his image on the phone.
And decision condemned.

Saheb Ghosh

Saheb Ghosh, a poet who loves nature very much. He believes in simplicity and he also indisputably believes that God is the reason of all reasons. He writes poem, essay and short story both in English and Bengali.

Waiting for You

How much I love, you can see
Your face like the shining moon charms me.
Your glamorous figure can attract anyone,
But you response me, except no one.

Now you are in far distance;
But every moment I can feel your presence.
I perceive your glinting eyes, when I remember you;
It seems that I am touching you.

For you, I can leave any important work,
My heart like a dog, continues to bark.
When will you come to appease my bustling heart,
In your love, again, I am waiting to dart.

Bushra Shaikh

Bushra Shaikh is a 21-year-old girl from Mumbai. She is studying physiotherapy. She likes to read and write. She is good at sports as well.

Tere Bin Tanha Yaha

Mein yaha ho kar bhi hu nhi
Mein jaha hun waha tu nhi
Mein hosh mein nhi hu
Teri mehfilon main mein nhi
Kya ye ajeeb nhi
Tu khush hai mere bina
Par mein toh tanha hu tere bina
Aalg hi haal hai aalg hi jazbaat hai
Ye kaisi tadap hai
Ye kaisi halchal hai
Tere bina tanha hu mein aur tu jane na
Ye kaisi tadap hai
Mein yaha ho kar bhi hu nhi
Mein jaha hu waha tu nhi

Flairs Et Glairs

Flairs and Glairs, a platform by a student for the students. We are esteemed youth struggling to carve out our path for our future and we follow a basic mindset Since everyone is not born with all-round skills. Joining hands with people who are born to execute it with perfection is the best way to evolve. Self-Evolution is the need of the hour but, evolving as a community is what we strive for. The initiative as kickstarted by, Founder- Mr. Shubham Shah with the motive to utilize the skillset and talent of writing has now a team of 10+ people who are actively participating into newer forms of learning and discovering talents among youngsters. We Provide platform and services like Publishing opportunities, Open mics, Workshops, Hands-on training. Operating with Brand Name Of Flairs and Glairs (Publication House), we offer the chance of elevating a passionate writer to an esteemed author With Brand name Teekhe Zasbaaat, We bring to you an opportunity to get accustomed with the Public Speaking and Presenting of Thoughts along with regular challenges to brush up your inking spirit. The newest initiative to extend our services we introduced in a new writing Platform- The Glittering Fables and Ink Over Tears.

We Choose to Fly Like A Falcon than to be a Leg Pulling Crab.

To Know More: Infoline – 7781900870
Mail Us At-
flairsandglairs@gmail.com / info@flairsandglairs.in
Or Visit is at
www.flairsandglairs.com / www.flairsandglairs.in
Social Handles- @flairsandglairs @teekhezasbaaat

www.ingramcontent.com/pod-product-compliance
Ingram Content Group UK Ltd.
Pitfield, Milton Keynes, MK11 3LW, UK
UKHW022005190726
13853UKWH00004B/1742

9 789390 416851